LOVESICK

LOVESICK

Poems by
GERALD STERN

PERENNIAL LIBRARY

HARPER & ROW, PUBLISHERS, New York

Cambridge, Philadelphia, San Francisco, Washington, London

Mexico City, São Paulo, Singapore, Sydney

Portions of this work originally appeared in *The American Poetry Review, The Nation, Three Rivers Poetry Journal, New England Review and Breadloaf Quarterly, Paris Review,* and *Pequod.*

"I Sometimes Think of a Lamb," "The Day," and "This Was a Wonderful Night" originally appeared in *The Bread Loaf Anthology of Contemporary American Poetry,* edited by Robert Pack, Sydney Lea, and Jay Parini, published by the University Press of New England.

FIRST EDITION

Designer: Ruth Bornschlegel
Copyeditor: Antonia Rachiele

Library of Congress Cataloging-in-Publication Data
Stern, Gerald.
  Lovesick.
  I. Title.
PS3569.T3888L6   1987   811'.54   86-46102
ISBN 0-06-055071-6   87 88 89 90 91 10 9 8 7 6 5 4 3 2 1
ISBN 0-06-096170-8 (pbk.)   87 88 89 90 91 10 9 8 7 6 5 4 3 2 1

For Diane Freund

Contents

LOVESICK

NOBODY ELSE LIVING

Nobody else living knows that song as well as I do.
On bad days I fill the tub with hot water
and rest my head on the freezing porcelain.
I fill the courtyard with sounds.
They come through the frosted glass,
they come through the transom. All that wonderful pity,
all that broken bliss, for twenty or thirty minutes
now rich and reminiscent and warm,
now cloudy and haunted.

LOVESICK

The dead straw in those trees, the
dead leaves in those trees
have turned to birds, they have turned
to crows, they are watching a deer
or a piece of tire, my foot
is on the deer's black head,
my face is in the clouds,
I kick the tire over
to see the guts. I want
the whole thing for myself.
They want the eyes, they want
the stinking shoulder, they wait
for me to leave, I kick
the legs, I drag them across
the highway, all those beaks
are snapping, all those tails
are waving in the wind,
their bellies are moaning and howling,
their souls are cooing and cawing.

ALL I HAVE ARE THE TRACKS

All I have are the tracks. There were a dog's
going down the powdered steps, there was a woman
going one way, a man going the other, a squirrel
on top of the man; sometimes his paws were firm,
the claws were showing—in fear, in caution—sometimes
they sort of scurried, then sort of leaped. The prints
go east and west; there is a boot; there is
a checkerboard style, a hexagram style; my own
I study now, my Georgia Loggers, the heel
a kind of target, the sole a kind of sponge;
the tiny feet are hopping, four little paws,
the distance between them is fifteen inches, they end
in the grass, in the leaves, there are four toes and a palm,
the nose isn't there, the tail isn't there, the teeth
that held the acorn, the eyes that thought; and the hands
that held the books, and the face that froze, and the shoulders
that fought the wind, and the mouth that struggled for air,
and love and hate, and all their shameless rages.

I DO A PIECE FROM GREECE

I do a piece from Greece. I haven't done that
for three or four years. I turn the radio up.
I stare at my ties. I pick a California
and wrap it around my robe. There is a shark
on the ceiling above my shoes. Her nose is pointed
toward the door. She is the streamlined body
we dreamed about in the thirties. Her tail is monstrous,
her brain is a pea. I pluck the strings
in a kind of serenade. I raise the bow
above my head and bend a little, my hair
is hanging down. I am at last the musician
my mother wanted. My aunts and uncles are sitting
on wooden boxes, they are sobbing and sighing,
I take my time, I have a Schubert to go.
I have a light beside me. I am lying
under the Sea of Azov, it is a joy
to be here, they are howling. I raise my elbow
to make a sound. I wait for the moon to shine
on the Allegheny. I look at their faces, they turn
the pages, eleven uncles and aunts, a leather
coffin. I start to play, it is the only
way I have of weeping, it is my way
of joining them, my tears were taken away
when I was eight, this way we end up singing
together. I am a note above them, it is
the thirteenth century, singing in fifths, in parts
of the south they sing like that; the violin rises
above the alto, a shrieking sound, we humans
shriek at the end, we want so much to be heard.
My way was with the soaring and the singing.
Once I heard it I could never stop.

I HATE MY MOANING

I hate my staring. I hate my moaning. Sometimes
I lie there in the morning arguing
against myself. I hold a mirror up
above the telephone so I can snip
a long hair from my eye. I balance a cup
of coffee on my stomach. Sometimes I sing,
sometimes I hold a feather against my nose,
sometimes I prop the clock against my ear,
sometimes I drag the speakers across the floor
and turn the volume up. There is a hole
above my head, the plaster is dropping, the lath
is exposed; there is a blanket over the window;
I hold it up with nails, it tears in the center
and lets a stream of light in; I can tell
when it's six o'clock, and seven o'clock, it is
my hour, the blanket is full of holes, the light
comes through the threads, it is a a greyish light,
perfect for either love or bitterness,
no exaggeration or deceit.

THIS WAS A WONDERFUL NIGHT

This was a wonderful night. I heard the Brahms
piano quintet, I read a poem by Schiller,
I read a story, I listened to *Gloomy Sunday*.
No one called me, I studied the birthday poem
of Alvaro de Campos. I thought, if there was time,
I'd think of my garden—all that lettuce, wasted,
all those huge tomatoes lying on the ground
rotting, and I'd think of the sticks I put there,
waving goodbye, those bearded sticks. De Campos,
he was the one who suffered most, his birthday
was like a knife to him; he sat in a chair
remembering his aunts; he thought of the flowers
and cakes, he thought of the sideboard crowded with gifts.
I look at the photo of Billie Holiday;
I turn the light bulb on and off. I envy
those poets who loved their childhood, those who remember
the extra places laid out, the china and glasses.
They want to devour the past, they revel in pity,
they live like burnt-out matches, memory ruins them;
again and again they go back to the first place.

De Campos and I are sitting on a bench
in some American city. He hardly knows
how much I love his country. I have two things
to tell him about my childhood, one is the ice
on top of the milk, one is the sign in the window—
three things—the smell of coal. There is some snow
left on the street, the wind is blowing. He trembles
and touches the buttons on his vest. His house
is gone, his aunts are dead, the tears run down

our cheeks and chins, we are like babies, crying.
"Leave thinking to the head," he says. I sob,
"I don't have birthdays any more," I say,
"I just go on," although I hardly feel
the sadness, there is such joy in being there
on that small bench, watching the sycamores,
looking for birds in the snow, listening for boots,
staring at the begonias, getting up
and down to rub the leaves and touch the buds—
endless pleasure, talking about New York,
comparing pain, writing the names down
of all the cities south of Lisbon, singing
one or two songs—a hundred years for him,
a little less for me, going east and west
in the new country, my heart forever pounding.

I SOMETIMES THINK OF THE LAMB

I sometimes think of the lamb when I crawl down
my flight of stairs, my back is twisted sideways
in a great arc of pain from the shoulder down
and the buttocks up. I think of the lamb through my tears
as I go down a step at a time, my left hand
squeezing the rail, my right hand holding my thigh
and lifting it up. As long as there is a lamb
I can get on my hands and knees if I have to
and walk across the floor like a limp wolf,
and I can get my body to the sink
and lift myself up to the white porcelain.
As long as there is a lamb, as long as he lives
in his brown pen or his green meadow,
as long as he kneels on the platform staring at the light,
surrounded by men and women with raised fingers,
as long as he has that little hump on his rear
and that little curve to his tail, as long as his foot
steps over the edge in terror and ignorance,
as long as he holds a cup to his own side,
as long as he is stabbed and venerated,
as long as there are hooves—and clattering—
as long as there is screaming and butchering.

STOPPING SCHUBERT

Stopping Schubert, ejecting him, changing the power,
I make it from Newark to the shores of Oberlin
in less than nine hours, Schubert roaring and groaning
halfway there, the violins in the mountains,
the cellos in the old state forests.
When I reach Clarion I know I am near Pittsburgh.
I turn the tape down; I can live off the music
of childhood for a while—I still know the words
in both languages—I am not that different
even today. My mouth makes a humming sound
just as it did back then. I take my comb out
and my piece of paper. I bang the swollen dashboard
thinking of my golden trombone; I ruined
the lives of twenty-four families in those days
sliding from note to note, it was my fate
not to make a sound on the French Horn,
to rage on my trombone. I still love Schubert
most of all, *Youth and the Maiden, Frozen Tears,*
Der Lindenbaum.
I have kept it a secret for forty years,
the tortured composer from central Pennsylvania,
Franz Schubert.

I AM IN A WINDOW

I move from chair to chair. Thinking of Liszt.
I am in a certain century again
going from city to city. I am in a window
with Berlioz on my left and Czerny on my right;
Liszt is looking into the clouds, his wrists
seem to be waiting. I am in an oil painting.
Victor Hugo is there, and Paganini,
and Sand and Dumas side by side. A bust
of Beethoven is half sitting on the piano,
half sitting in the sky. We live by the light
of Saint-Simon—it is our socialism,
freedom from rage, freedom from marriage,
freedom from money; or it is Weimar
forty years later, Liszt is at the window,
Wagner has come and gone, the world is whistling
Brahms and Debussy; in a few years
Gandhi will be born, then Frank Lloyd Wright.
The continent has shifted half an inch,
a little joy has come to Zuyder Zee,
a little horror has come to the Crimea.
I move from table to table, from room to room,
I try to think of Gurdjieff, what was the work
he had in store for me? Where were the shovels?
I think of Rudolf Steiner, all the reading
he did on Hegel and Goethe; I think of the gatherings
in Switzerland, and France, I see his hand
in a book, his eyes are radiant. I pack
my bag, a leather strap, a leather pocket—
how well the goods were made in 1910,
fifteen years before my birth—my soul

was probably born too late, it had a certain
zest, I think, for the wrong century
and fluttered along for decade after decade
with the wrong digits—that is the way it is
with souls—I have a rug upstairs to roll in,
something to keep me warm, it came from Crete
and has three green and yellow flowers on it,
on a field of crimson; I bought it in Chania.
I'll lie there for hours thinking of my mountains,
reading Keats.

BÉLA

This version of the starving artist
has him composing his last concerto
while dying of leukemia. Serge Koussevitsky
visits him in his hospital room
with flowers in his hand, the two of them
talk in tones of reverence, the last
long piece could be the best, the rain somewhere
makes daring noises, somewhere clouds are bursting.
I have the record in front of me. I drop
the needle again on the famous ending, five
long notes, then all is still, I have to imagine
two great seconds of silence and then applause
and shouting, he is in tears, Koussevitsky
leads him onto the stage. Or he is distant,
remembering the mountains, there in Boston
facing the wild Americans, he closes
his eyes so he can hear another note,
something from Turkey, or Romania, his mother
holding his left hand, straightening out the fingers,
he bows from the waist, he holds his right hand up.
I love the picture with Benny Goodman, Szigetti
is on the left, Goodman's cheeks are puffed
and his legs are crossed. Bartók is at the piano.
They are rehearsing Bartók's *Contrasts*. I lift
my own right hand, naturally I do that;
I listen to my blood, I touch my wrist.
If he could have only lived for three more years
he could have heard about our Mussolini
and seen the violent turn to the right and the end
of one America and the beginning of another.

That would have given him time enough to brood
on Hungary; that would have given him time
also to go among the Indians
and learn their music, and listen to their chants,
those tribes from Michigan and Minnesota,
just like the tribes of the Finns and the Urgo-Slavics,
moaning and shuffling in front of their wooden tents.

There is a note at the end of the second movement
I love to think about; it parodies
Shostakovitch; it is a kind of flutter
of the lips. And there is a note—I hear it—
of odd regret for a life not lived enough,
everyone knows that sound, for me it's remorse,
and there is a note of crazy satisfaction,
this I love, of the life he would not change
no matter what—no other animal
could have such pleasure. I think of this as I turn
the music off, and I think of his poor eyes
as they turned to ice—his son was in the room
and saw the change—I call it a change. Bartók
himself lectured his friends on death, it was
his woods and mountain lecture, fresh green shoots
pushing up through the old, the common home
that waits us all, the cycles, the laws of nature,
wonderfully European, all life and death
at war—peacefully—one thing replacing another,
although he grieved over cows and pitied dogs
and listened to pine cones as if they came from the sea
and fretted over the smallest of life.
                                        He died
September 28, 1945,
just a month after the war was over.
It took him sixty days to finish the piece
from the time he lay there talking to Koussevitsky
to the time he put a final dot on the paper,

a little pool of ink to mark the ending.
There are the five loud notes, I walk upstairs
to hear them, I put a silk shawl over my head
and rock on the wooden floor, the shawl is from France
and you can see between the threads; I feel
the darkness, I was born with a veil over
my eyes, it took me forty years to rub
the gum away, it was a blessing, I sit
for twenty minutes in silence, daylight is coming,
the moon is probably near, probably lifting
its satin nightgown, one hand over the knee
to hold the cloth up so the feet can walk
through the wet clouds; I love that bent-over motion,
that grace at the end of a long and furious night.
I go to sleep on the floor, there is a pillow
somewhere for my heavy head, my hand
is resting on the jacket, Maazel is leading
the Munich orchestra, a nurse is pulling
the sheet up, Bartók is dead, his wife is walking
past the sun room, her face is white, her mind
is on the apartment they lost, where she would put
the rugs, how she would carry in his breakfast,
where they would read, her mind is on Budapest,
she plays the piano for him, she is eighteen
and he is thirty-seven, he is gone
to break the news, she waits in agony,
she goes to the telephone; I turn to the window,
I stare at my palm, I draw a heart in the dust,
I put the arrow through it, I place the letters
one inside the other. I sleep, I sleep.

A SONG FOR THE ROMEOS *

FOR MY BROTHERS
JIM WRIGHT AND DICK HUGO

I'm singing a song for the romeos
I wore for ten years on my front stoop in the North Side,
and for the fat belly I carried
and the magic ticket sticking out of my greasy hatband
or my vest pocket,
the green velvet one with the checkered borders
and the great stretched back with the tan ribs
going west and east like fishes of the deep looking for their
      covers.

I'm wearing my romeos
with the papery thin leather
and the elastic side bands.
They are made for sitting,
or a little walking into the kitchen and out,
a little tea in the hands,
a little Old Forester or a little Schenley in the tea.

I'm singing a song for the corner store
and the empty shelves;
for the two blocks of flattened buildings
and broken glass;
for the streetcar that still rounds the bend
with sparks flying through the air.

And the woman with a shopping bag,
and the girl with a book
walking home one behind the other,

* Romeos were a kind of indoor/outdoor slipper or sandal.

their steps half dragging, half ringing,
the romeos keeping time,
tapping and knocking and clapping on the wooden steps
and the cement sidewalk.

TASHLIKH*

This one shows me standing by the Delaware
for the last time. There is a book in one hand
and I am making cunning motions with the other,
chopping and weaving motions to illustrate
what I am reading, or I am just enlarging
the text with my hand the way a good Jew did
before the 1930s. I am wearing
a Russian cap and a black overcoat
I bought in Pittsburgh in 1978,
a *Cavalier*, from Kaufmann's, a gabardine
with bluish buttons. Behind me in the locusts
and up and down the banks are ten or twelve others
in coats and hats, with books in their hands. We sing
a song for the year and throw our sticks in the water.
We empty our pockets of paper and lint. I know
that there are fish there in the Delaware
so we are linked to the silver chain, and I know
that the fire is wet and sputtering, a fire
to rest your boots on, perfect for the smoke
to rise just a little and move an inch at a time
across the water. I throw another stick—
this one a maple—onto the greasy rocks
and climb the hill, the rubber steps and the saplings.
I make a kissing sound with my hand—I guess
we all do. This was a painful year, a painful

* An ancient Jewish ceremony in which sins, in the form of
bread, are cast into a body of running water. It is observed late in
the afternoon during the first day of Rosh Ha-Shanah. The core of
the ceremony is a recitation from Micah.

two years. It is a joy to be here, sailing
back and forth across the highway, smelling
one thing or another, not just living
in terror, sleeping again, and breathing.

PUSSY WILLOW

For fifty years I have rubbed these soft heads
against my face
and joined, this way, the men and women who stood
in the wet meadows and rubbed *their* faces for hours
with the brown fur.
I know they stared at each other with wet eyes
and opened their mouths from time to time in amazement.
I think of them either as looking at the sun
through shiny leaves or getting on their knees
to rub their necks with water. I think the fur
brought pity to them, it helped them live with the dead,
it helped the sound in their throats.
I think they must have come down from the mountains—
those who lived there—to find the ponds and creeks.
It could have been one of the first journeys
and there could have been songs and processions,
with musical bows and drums.
I somehow know it when I am looking at the sun
and rubbing my cheeks, when I am working my fingers
up the stems and snapping the heads off.
The sounds just come, the lovely throbbing and humming.

A SLOW AND PAINFUL RECOVERY

Richard Strauss, my hero, here you are
finally letting go of both sword and breast,
and there you are escaping from our bleeding world
onto a mountain or into a cloud. I stare
at the pink fixture, it is a flattened breast
with a longish nipple, breasts half over the world
are covering light bulbs, there is a light bulb out
and a darkened breast in the other room; I stay here
with my lilacs and daisies, I am in my bed
of needles. Now it's Schumann again, the second,
his deep depression gone by the final movement
and soon it will be Mozart, Europe again,
the true Europe, lilacs everywhere,
the cellos of the plant world. This is the last
good day for the first bouquet. I know there are some
daisies left among the lilies. The second
bouquet is better, it refuses to bow,
it brings the outside in, I think it's the bluebell,
I think it's the red bud crawling and twisting, a kind of
Japanese dancing, maybe more formal than twisting.

I'm writing the fourteenth now. I'm doing it
in a room with all my boxes and boots and paintings.
I'm getting ready to move. My bed of needles—
crooked, antique—is in the midst of it all.
Each day I walk a mile, I crawl and twist
like a broken branch, I pass the scented tree,
I pass the poppies, I pass the lilacs, I climb
two giant hills, my face is twisted, I hold
the rusted rail—this house is historical—

and pull myself up the steps. My crisis was the spine,
one or two flattened discs, I had the pain,
I had the depression, I had the boredom. There are
paths I know that no one knows. I know
the color of tulips in every yard. I know
the sheets of green with yellow discs. I watch them
turn white. I know a house so small the owners
are either midgets with squeaky voices or giants
with little chairs and tables, little beds
they and their children play in. There is a mailbox
nailed onto the shingles. There is a railing
falling over—the giants' heavy touch,
the midgets' swinging. There is a small backyard
with white and purple lilacs. I am listening
to Haydn's sixty-sixth, the ever loyal
Haydn, Haydn the good, Ben Franklin Haydn.
I take my pills—daily at bedtime—I look at
my Cretan rug. I fought for days to save
five or ten dollars, every day the dealer
sent out for coffee, every day he told me
about his life in Chicago and every day
we struggled in silence. I turn the lights out, my mind
is all alone, it begs for valium, it cries
for milk and scotch. At four in the morning the birds
and I are screaming. I start my long walk at five;
the shadows let me alone, the perfume tree
is silent, my hands are shaking—a little residual
weakness—my leg is dragging, I turn the corner
to a kind of dawn, there is a weak light over
the sycamores—the perfume tree is apple—
the red bud is split in two, the poppies are opening.
It was a slow and painful recovery.

MY FIRST KINGLET

I saw my first kinglet in Iowa City
on Sunday, April twenty-second, 1984,
flying from tree to tree, and bush to bush.
She had a small yellow patch on her stomach,
a little white around her eyes. I reached
for a kiss, still dumb and silent as always. I put
a finger out for a branch and opened my hand
for a kind of clearing in the woods, a wrinkled
nest you'd call it, half inviting, half
disgusting maybe, or terrifying, a pink
and living nest. The kinglet stood there singing
"A Mighty Fortress Is Our God." She was
a pure Protestant, warbling in the woods,
confessing everything. I said goodbye,
a friend of all the Anabaptists, a friend
of all the Lutherans. I cleared my throat
and off she went for some other pink finger
and some other wrinkled palm. I started to whistle,
but only to the trees; my kinglet was gone
and her pipe was gone and her yellow crown was gone,
and I was left with only a spiral notebook
and the end of a pencil. I was good and careful,
for all I had left of the soul was in that stub,
a wobbling hunk of lead embedded in wood,
pine probably—pencils are strange—I sang
another Protestant hymn; the lead was loose
and after a minute I knew I'd just be holding
the blunt and slippery end. That was enough
for one Sunday. I thanked the trees, I thanked
the tulips with their six red tongues. I lay

another hour, another hour; I either
slept a little or thought a little. Life—
it could have been a horror, it could have been
gory and full of pain. I ate my sandwich
and waited for a signal, then I began
my own confession; I walked on the stones, I sighed
under a hemlock, I whistled under a pine,
and reached my own house almost out of breath
from walking too fast—from talking too loud—
from waving my arms and beating my palms; I was,
for five or ten minutes, one of those madmen you see
forcing their way down Broadway, reasoning with themselves
the way a squirrel does, the way a woodpecker does,
half dressed in leaf, half dressed in light, my dear face
appearing and disappearing, my heavy legs
with their shortened hamstrings tripping a little, a yard
away from my wooden steps and my rusty rail,
the thicket I lived in for two years, more or less,
Dutch on one side, American Sioux on the other,
Puerto Rican and Bronx Hasidic inside,
a thicket fit for a king or a wandering kinglet.

I SLEPT LIKE THAT

It was always a soothing position,
holding my arm up with the elbow locked
and the fingers bent.
I was always a birch tree,
with a long curved bough and a limb hanging down
half touching the grass.
I slept like that
and dreamed of the light coming through and my five dry
        fingers
returning to life.
That was in Pittsburgh and New York and Trenton and
        Camden.
And Philadelphia. Philadelphia, P.A. . . .
I slept by the river—always—and followed the devious way.
In five old cities, each with an ancient and brutal government,
I lived with my arm in the sky and my fingers bent.

LILLIAN HARVEY

This is lovesick for you—Charles Koechlin
covering his paper with tears, he shushes his wife
and his children, he is crying for Lillian Harvey—
or this is lovesick—sending his wife to meet her,
he is too shy to go, and he is married;
when she comes back he asks a thousand questions:
What was she wearing? Does she like his music?
How old did she look? Was she like her photograph?
But he never met her, she whose face haunted him,
although he wrote a hundred and thirteen compositions
for her, including two *Albums for Lillian,*
and he wrote a film scenario and score,
which he imagined, fantastically,
would star the two of them. He was himself
twice in America, both times in California,
but they couldn't meet—it would be a violation.
I know that agony myself, I stood
on one foot or another four or five times
and burned with shame and shook with terror. You never
go yourself. I know he must have waited
outside her house, a crazy man, he must have
dialed her number a hundred times, even risked
his life for her. But you never go, you never
stand there smiling—he never stood there smiling,
he never reached his hand inside her dress,
he never touched her nipple, he never pressed
his mouth against her knee or lifted her thighs.
For she was the muse. You never fuck the muse.

THERE I WAS ONE DAY

There I was one day
in the parking lot of the First Brothers' Church
on one foot, a giant whooping crane
with my left ibex finger against my temple
trying to remember what my theory of corruption was
and why I got so angry years ago
at my poor mother and father, immigrant cranes
from Polish Russia and German and Jewish Ukraine—
the good days then, hopping both ways like a frog,
and croaking, and trying to remember why it was
I soothed myself with words
at that flimsy secretary, not meant for knees,
not meant for a soul, not least a human one,
and trying to remember how I pieced together
the great puzzle, and how delighted I was
I would never again be bitten twice,
on either hand, the left one or the other.
I stopped between the telephone pole and the ivy
and sang to myself. I do it now for pleasure.
I thought I'd trace the line of pure decadence
to either Frank Sinatra or Jackie Gleason,
and thence to either the desert or the swamp,
Greater Nevada or Miami Beach;
or I would smile with Stalin or frown with Frick,
Stalin and Frick, both from Pittsburgh; Mellon,
Ehrlichman, Paul the Fortieth, Paul the Fiftieth.
I learned my bitterness at the dining room table
and used it everywhere. One time I yanked
the tablecloth off with everything on top of it.
It was the kind of strength that lets you lift

the back end of a car, it was the rush
of anger and righteousness you shake from later.
My Polish mother and my Ukrainian father
sat there white-faced. They had to be under fifty,
maybe closer to forty. I had hit them
between the eyes, I had screamed in their ears
and spit in their faces. Forty years later I stutter
when I think about it; it is the stuttering
of violent justice. I turned left on Third—
it was called Pomfret in 1776—
and made my way to the square—I think I did that—
past the Plaza II and the old Huntington,
and did an Egyptian turn. There were some other birds
sitting there on the benches, eating egg salad
and smoking autumn leaves. They didn't seem to care
or even notice. We sat there for the humming
and later we left, one at a time, and limped
away at different speeds, in different directions.
I ended up doing a circle, east on one street,
north on another, past the round oak table
in the glass window, past the swimming pool
at the YW. Just a walk for me
is full of exhaustion; nobody does it my way,
shaking the left foot, holding the right foot up,
a stork from Broadway, a heron from Mexico,
a pink flamingo from Greece.

ONE ANIMAL'S LIFE

FOR ROSALIND PACE

This is how I saved one animal's life,
I raised the lid of the stove and lifted the hook
that delicately held the cheese—I think it was bacon—
so there could be goodness and justice under there.
It was a thirty-inch range with the pilot lit
in the center of two small crosses. It was a Wincroft
with a huge oven and two flat splash pans above it.
The four burners were close together, it was
a piece of white joy, from 1940 I'd judge
from the two curved handles, yet not as simple as
my old Slattery, not as sleek. I owe
a lot to the woman who gave me this house, she is
a lover of everything big and small, she moans
for certain flowers and insects, I hear her snuffle
all night sometimes, I hear her groan. She gave me
a bed and a kitchen, she gave me music, I couldn't be
disloyal to her, yet I had to lift
the murderous hook. I'll hear her lectures later
on *my* inconsistencies and hypocrisies;
I'll struggle in the meantime, like everyone else, to make
my way between the stove and refrigerator
without sighing or weeping too much. Mice
are small and ferocious. If I killed one it wouldn't be
with poison or traps. I couldn't just use our weapons
without some compensation. I'd have to be present—
if it was a trap—and hear it crash and lift
the steel myself and look at the small flat nose
or the small crushed head, I'd have to hold the pallet
and drop the body into a bag. I ask
forgiveness of butchers and hunters; I'm starting to talk

28

to vegetarians now, I'm reading books,
I'm washing my icebox down with soda and lye,
I'm buying chicory, I'm storing beans.
I should have started this thirty years ago,
holding my breath, eating ozone, starving,
sitting there humming, feeling pure and indignant
beside the chewed-up bags and the black droppings.

SILVER HAND

There is that little silver hand. I wrap
my fingers around the wrist. I press my thumb
on the shiny knuckles. There is a little slot
in the empty palm—the lines are crude and lifeless,
more like an ape's hand, more like a child's, no hope
for the future of any kind, a life line dragging
its way through civilization, the line of destiny
faint and broken, a small abandoned road,
the heart line short, no sweetness, no ecstasy,
and no dear journeys, and no great windfalls. I shake
the wrist, there are some dimes and nickels inside,
but it is mostly empty, an empty hand
reaching out. It is the hand that acts
for the spirit, there is a connection, the hand has mercy,
the hand is supple and begs, the hand is delicate,
even if it is brutal sometimes, even if it is evil—
and it is penniless and lost, a true
spirit, that sings a little and dances a little,
green or shiny on the outside, black on the inside.
Give to the hand!

WASHINGTON SQUARE

Now after all these years I am just that one pigeon
limping over towards that one sycamore tree
with my left leg swollen and my left claw bent and my neck
just pulling me along. It is the annual
day of autumn glory, but I am limping
into the shade of that one sycamore tree.
Forget about Holley crumbling out there in the square,
forget about Garibaldi in his little hollow;
remember one pigeon, white and grey, with a touch
of the old blue, his red leg swollen, his claw
dragging him on and on, the sickness racking
his skinny neck; remember the one pigeon
fighting his way through the filthy marijuana,
sighing.

ARRANGING A THORN

I am wandering through Newark, New Jersey,
among the gymnasts, the accountants and the kings
and my arms are breaking from all the weight I carry.
I am wearing the same blue pants and jacket
I have worn for the last twenty years
and mumbling to myself as always
as I go out of one long corridor and into another
or up an escalator
and into a jazzy bar
or through the beeper, over and over again,
discarding my metal, dropping my keys and watches.
I am ranked below the businessmen
with their two-suiters and their glasses of ice
and I get a slightly bored or slightly disdainful look
from the flight attendants and the drunken crew
and the food gatherers.
This is the trip I'm going to think about Rexroth
and what it was like in 1959
reading his poem on murdered poets,
and Shelley's *Adonais*
and Dunbar's *Lament*,
half a dirge for Dunbar,
half a dirge for the reader, sick and dying.
—Ah brother Levine and brother Stanley Plumly,
what hell we live in; we travel from Tuscaloosa
to Houston; we go to Chicago; we meet the monster
and spend our night at the Richmont or the Hyatt,
there is a table by the bed, the rug
on the wall is there to ruin us, coffee and toast
is seven dollars. Murphy meets us in leather

at the South Street station and drives us over a curb;
I pay for my own meal; twenty people show up
for the reading; it is the night that Carter loses;
my back is out of place. It was in the *Ion*
that Plato doomed the poets. There is no peace
in any land, we stand in the dust and kick
our shoes, some with holes in the toes and some
with holes in the soles. That's all there is. The prizes
are there for delusion. Oh brother Ignatow, oh br'er
Bly, there is such joy in sitting here knowing
one thing from another; I feel like singing;
that darkness is gone, that angry blackness. I sort
the leaves, my life is full of leaves again,
I make a garland for my head, it is
a garland of pity—I won't say glory—poets
are full of pity, I talk to them, they hate to
think about glory, it is the terror, everything
lost, their poems shredded and burned, their music
boring, or insignificant, or derivative,
a critic somewhere keeping time, but *pity*,
pity is for this life, pity is the worm
inside the meat, pity is the meat, pity
is the shaking pencil, pity is the shaking voice—
not enough money, not enough love—pity
for all of us—it is our grace, walking
down the ramp or on the moving sidewalk,
sitting in a chair, reading the paper, pity,
turning a leaf to the light, arranging a thorn.

THE DOG

What I was doing with my white teeth exposed
like that on the side of the road I don't know,
and I don't know why I lay beside the sewer
so that lover of dead things could come back
with his pencil sharpened and his piece of white paper.
I was there for a good two hours whistling
dirges, shrieking a little, terrifying
hearts with my whimpering cries before I died
by pulling the one leg up and stiffening.
There is a look we have with the hair of the chin
curled in mid-air, there is a look with the belly
stopped in the midst of its greed. The lover of dead things
stoops to feel me, his hand is shaking. I know
his mouth is open and his glasses are slipping.
I think his pencil must be jerking and the terror
of smell—and sight—is overtaking him;
I know he has that terrified faraway look
that death brings—he is contemplating. I want him
to touch my forehead once and rub my muzzle
before he lifts me up and throws me into
that little valley. I hope he doesn't use
his shoe for fear of touching me; I know,
or used to know, the grasses down there; I think
I knew a hundred smells. I hope the dog's way
doesn't overtake him, one quick push,
barely that, and the mind freed, something else,
some other thing, to take its place. Great heart,
great human heart, keep loving me as you lift me,
give me your tears, great loving stranger, remember
the death of dogs, forgive the yapping, forgive

the shitting, let there be pity, give me your pity.
How could there be enough? I have given
my life for this, emotion has ruined me, oh lover,
I have exchanged my wildness—little tricks
with the mouth and feet, with the tail, my tongue is a parrot's,
I am a rampant horse, I am a lion,
I wait for the cookie, I snap my teeth—
as you have taught me, oh distant and brilliant and lonely.

SHAKING MYSELF AND SIGHING

What a sweet urinal it was in Narbonne,
the smoke coming up in the form of thin wisps,
the tough little roots sticking out above our eyes.
You could hear music there, something that
wailed and something that snorted, it was a
perfect place for sound. I touched the stone
above my head with the flat of my hand, it was
the right hand, elbow bent and forehead almost
touching the roots. I hummed a little and listened
to cars on the wall. Pleasure would drag me down
to the wide canal and fate would drag me through
the five hundred years of silt. My eyes would water
thinking of the Saracens or thinking
of the Jews arriving from Spain and Africa
with books and shawls. I thought of Moses Khimki,
the Blue Book mentions him; I thought of the Jewry
leaving their city forever, going down to Poitiers,
going back to Barcelona, I stood there sighing,
shaking myself and sighing. If I had stayed
I would have come back in 1960, half
a scholar, half a poet. I would have spent
two years teaching in Perpignan, I would have
lived in Carcassonne, I would have walked
the road from Montpellier to Sête again
and spent another Thanksgiving there, still dreaming
of renting a boat—with two or three others—still singing
American songs, among the Phoenicians,
visiting Valery's grave, bicycling back
to Montpellier at two, or three, in the morning,
singing in French, or being silent. I would have

done that three or four times. God forgive me
for coming back, there I am standing and talking
to two or three Arabs—we kiss—there I am sitting
at six A.M. across from the park; I have
a roll in my right hand, I have lifted the blessed
coffee to my lips, God forgive me
for my desertion—I am a heavy moaner,
can that be forgiven?—I owe a song to Basnight,
he lived in Turkey for twenty years; I owe
a song to Brett, he lived in Greece for almost
twenty-five years. I would have packed my silver
in straw, I would have packed my books in paper
and dropped the key inside the lion's mouth
and left when the chairs and cushions were still burning.

A PAIR OF HANDS

That is a pair of white hands I see
floating in the mirror, the fingers on the left
are blunt and rounded, the ones on the right are raised
as if in thought. They are almost like gloves,
the lines are gone, they are abstracted, the suffering
is in the creases, somewhere in the folds
underneath the knuckles, or somewhere in the spaces
over the fingertips. I choose them this time
over the mouth, the mouth with two great trenches
and two great cheeks beyond the trenches, the mouth
with a curled smile, and I choose them over the eyes,
surrounded by wrinkles, wounded and bloodshot. The hands
are permanent and heavy, they are the means
both to pain and pleasure, thus the ancient
Peruvians buried them inside their clothes,
thus the Arabs cut them off and fed
them to their dogs. Our age is weak—and vague—
in what it does with hands, there is a history
both of terror and loathing. My first forty years
were an agony. I lived by touching and holding.
It was my ruin.

BOB SUMMERS' BODY

I never told this—I saw Bob Summers' body
one last time when they dropped him down the chute
at the crematorium. He turned over twice
and seemed to hang with one hand to the railing
as if he had to sit up once and scream
before he reached the flames. I was half terrified
and half ashamed to see him collapse like that
just two minutes after we had sung for him
and said our pieces. It was impossible
for me to see him starting another destiny
piled up like that, or see him in that furnace
as one who was being consoled or purified.
If only we had wrapped him in his sheet
so he could be prepared; there is such horror
standing before Persephone with a suit on,
the name of the manufacturer in the lining,
the pants too short, or too long. How hard it was
for poor Bob Summers in this life, how he struggled
to be another person. I hope his voice,
which he lost through a stroke in 1971,
was given back to him, wherever he strayed,
the smell of smoke still on him, the fire lighting up
his wonderful eyes again, his hands explaining,
anyone, god or man, moved by his logic,
spirits in particular, saved by the fire and clasping
their hands around their knees, some still worm-bound,
their noses eaten away, their mouths only dust,
nodding and smiling in the plush darkness.

IT WAS IN HOUSTON

It was in Houston I saw this disgusting sideboard
with dogs and foxes and lobsters carved into
the wood, a giant stag was hanging down
from a polished rope, there was an eagle on top
and bowls of fruit and plates of fish—all carved.
I opened the drawer and put my message inside.
The drawer was smooth and faultless, one of the hidden
ones without knobs, curved and rounded, with nice
round insides that soothe the soul. It might
take a year for someone to open the drawer.
It would be either a mother or her son;
the mother would be mad with cleaning, her fingers
would itch to get at the inside of that furniture
and rub some oil into the corners, the son
would long to take the piece apart, to loosen
the stag, to free the eagle, to find a dime
inside the hidden drawer. This would be before
she turned to books and he turned to motorcycles;
or it would be a musician, someone who loves
to touch old wood. It never would be a poet—
they are all blind—who pulls the drawer and finds
my secret words. For any of these three,
here is the white pen I am writing with,
here is my yellow tablet, there are no
magic thumb prints, nothing that is not there,
only the hum, and I have buried that
on the piece of paper. It is a small envelope;
I always have one in my jacket; the words
are simple, half music, half thought, half tongue, half tear,
and made for the pocket book or the hip pocket,

or the inside of a wallet—I like that best—
folded up, and there are broken words,
or torn, hanging onto the threads, the deep ones
underneath the flap, the dark ones forever creased,
the song half hovering in that cloth lining
as if a moth were struggling out of the leather,
half caught between the money and the poetry,
little white one in the ravaged world.

NEITHER ENGLISH NOR SPANISH

FOR HEIDI KALAFSKI

It was when I went out to get an angry soul
a little cool and a little windy. Some bird
was clacking his beak or maybe rubbing his gums
together either for singing or for crushing
a watery insect. I was driving with one sister
to find another and the car we drove in
was huge and fast and dangerous. I thought
the darkness we drove in was something like daylight
        although
the lights on the body seemed more like lamps, just lighting
the ten or twelve feet in front of us. It is
the madness of northern New Jersey I'm describing,
a sulphur day and night, a cloud of gas
always hanging above us. We drifted down
to Newark, there were clusters of people in front of
every bar and drug store, they were mostly
very young, as if the population over twenty
had disappeared and the care of life and the care of
the culture were in the hands of babies, all our
wisdom, our history, were in their hands. I stopped
over and over to ask directions, the language
they spoke was neither English nor Spanish, they either
pointed in some odd direction or stood there staring.
I bounced up over the curb into a radiant
gasoline island; there was a psycho-pomp
in a clean white suit who calmed me down and told me
where the phone booth and the park was I wanted.
His English was perfect. I was shocked to see him
in a job like that, reaching over and wiping
the mist away, holding his hand on the pump,

staring at nothing. He should have been a lawyer
or engineer, but he was black, although
he could have been a student. I gave him a tip
and turned around. This time I found the park
in half a minute but there was nothing in sight,
not even a police car with its fat dog yowling
or some stray bleak berserker on the burnt grass.
I locked the car, the other sister sat there
trembling. I tried to smile. I found a dime,
and then a quarter, for my phone call. I stood there
on the sidewalk holding the black receiver
and listening to noisy insects. The sweet life
outside is different from the life of the car.
I suddenly wanted to walk. I wanted to touch
the trees, or sit on the ground. There was a ringing
but no one answered, as I recall. I shouldn't
have made a mystique of that but I was shouting
"bad connection" to myself and "vile connection"
and "fake connection," all that we hold dear
in twentieth-century evil communication.
That was where I could have lifted my fist
and played for the dirty trees, but I was tired
and struggling with the stupid lock, a Ford
Galaxy Superba. Anyhow, I got bored
with the park and its shadows, I did a fainthearted dance,
a mild frenzy on the sidewalk, and sang me
a primitive note, a long moaning note,
as I put my car into "drive," the lever hanging
somewhere in oblivion, the meshes
ruined, no right connection between the orange
letters and the mushy gears.
                                    This was
my futile descent into Newark. We returned
empty-handed, empty-hearted. I smoked
a single cigarette in the blackness and ranted
against New Jersey, as if there was a difference

between one land and another. That dear girl
we looked for would be sitting in the kitchen,
surrounded by her family, thin and exhausted,
full of terror, her mind erasing one horror
after another; and I would hold her and kiss her
along with the others. We would be some tragic
group somewhere, someone would boil water,
and we would talk all night, even end up laughing
a little before the streaks of light and the morning
noises brought us to our senses. I turned
right where I had to turn right and found the buried
driveway as always. I was right, the kitchen
lights were burning and there were cars and trucks
parked wildly in the yard. I looked at the dawn
behind the A&P and the pizzeria—
that takes two seconds in New Jersey—and climbed
over a sled, a tire and an ironing board—
I who saw the dead and knew the music—
and opened the door to that embattled kitchen
and shook hands all around, I and the sister.

I AM IN LOVE

Everyone who dances understands what I am doing,
standing for hours in front of the card catalogue
and walking up and down the black riverbank.
He understands it how I stop and gesture,
that talking to the dead, and how I make
a face for every age, a vile one for ours,
a sweet one for one I half forgot, a wrinkled one
for the one that is Peruvian and a smooth one
for the one that is Egyptian. I have been working
among the O's; I started with Orpheus
and have been there for months; there are some libraries
where you can live in the stacks, you bring your lunch
and sleep on the heated floor. My scholarship
is hectic, I can start with an O and stray
to everything in sight, Pound and paideuma,
Palladio—I steal that from my son—
his trips through Italy, his view of the sky.
There is a dance in which I sit for one hour
with warm milk in my hands, the furnace is roaring
and just outside the window one or two cars
are driving by in the darkness. In it I either
find a book, or I find a piece of paper
and a yellow pencil. I sway a little and moan
all to myself. When I am done, when the milk
is done, I stand and bow to the shopping bag,
to the Sears rug—I have an audience—
and climb the fifteen steps with my head down
and my legs dragging—another dance. I have
a helpless fascination with myself,
I love to watch myself when I climb stairs,

or when I drink that milk. I stay alive
that way, I am amazed at myself. I have
no power over it, whether I'm lying and sleeping
or lying awake and staring. Sometimes I sit
like a stone, I do the lines of wind and rain,
sometimes I do the birch tree searching for the sun,
sometimes I do Route 30. I am in love.

MY FAVORITE DEMON

My favorite demon holds me by the hair
and gnaws behind my ear. Though one hand digs
into my neck, the other holds my head
almost lovingly and her deep frown
is only the frown of concentration. My lips
are full and red and my face is gaunt. My eyes
are closed as if to receive the pain. A tear,
always the tiny symbol, rests on the bridge
before descending, as it must, to the valley
between the cheek and the lip, or sometimes even
down to the tip of the nose. There is a tail
somewhere out in front and a pair of horns
protruding from the lobes, although her face
is human, and aside from the gnawing and sucking
she is almost kind. My own joy was
walking and thinking. I had a fascination
with secret knowledge. Also I sighed and moaned.
Also I hated controversy. Mostly
I was slow in learning and slow in changing,
but that had nothing to do with chewing and gnawing—
at least I think not. If anything it was
the closeness I loved, as ludicrous as that sounds,
and if we chose each other, if I chose her,
if she chose me, it was for the closeness. Imagine
calling that love, the skin ripped off and the red
bones exposed, such wild distortion, my head
half rolling, half bouncing, imagine my eyes, imagine
them pleading, imagine my screaming, I, the soul
of sanity, caught up in violence and sorrow.

ANOTHER INSANE DEVOTION

This was gruesome—fighting over a ham sandwich
with one of the tiny cats of Rome, he leaped
on my arm and half hung on to the food and half
hung on to my shirt and coat. I tore it apart
and let him have his portion, I think I lifted him
down, sandwich and all, on the sidewalk and sat
with my own sandwich beside him, maybe I petted
his bony head and felt him shiver. I have
told this story over and over; some things
root in the mind; his boldness, of course, was frightening
and unexpected—his stubbornness—though hunger
drove him mad. It was the breaking of boundaries,
the sudden invasion, but not only that, it was
the sharing of food and the sharing of space; he didn't
run into an alley or into a cellar,
he sat beside me, eating, and I didn't run
into a trattoria, say, shaking,
with food on my lips and blood on my cheek, sobbing;
but not only that, I had gone there to eat
and wait for someone. I had maybe an hour
before she would come and I was full of hope
and excitement. I have resisted for years
interpreting this, but now I think I was given
a clue, or I was giving myself a clue,
across the street from the glass sandwich shop.
That was my last night with her, the next day
I would leave on the train for Paris and she would
meet her husband. Thirty-five years ago
I ate my sandwich and moaned in her arms, we were
dying together; we never met again

although she was pregnant when I left her—I have
a daughter or son somewhere, darling grandchildren
in Norwich, Connecticut, or Canton, Ohio.
Every five years I think about her again
and plan on looking her up. The last time
I was sitting in New Brunswick, New Jersey,
and heard that her husband was teaching at Princeton,
if she was still married, or still alive, and tried
calling. I went that far. We lived
in Florence and Rome. We rowed in the bay of Naples
and floated, naked, on the boards. I started
to think of her again today. I still
am horrified by the cat's hunger. I still
am puzzled by the connection. This is another
insane devotion, there must be hundreds, although
it isn't just that, there is no pain, and the thought
is fleeting and sweet. I think it's my own dumb boyhood,
walking around with Slavic cheeks and burning
stupid eyes. I think I gave the cat
half of my sandwich to buy my life, I think
I broke it in half as a decent sacrifice.
It was this I bought, the red coleus,
the split rocking chair, the silk lampshade.
Happiness. I watched him with pleasure.
I bought memory. I could have lost it.
How crazy it sounds. His face twisted with cunning.
The wind blowing through his hair. His jaws working.

THE BLINK OF AN EYE

Twilight is like the blink of an eye;
this one comes in and this one goes out
and it is impossible to grasp.
I stand with day behind me and night ahead.
There is the sun and there is the moon, both moving
across the sky. I stretch my hand for silence
before I put my fingers up to straddle
the two orbs. If I can bend down I'll touch
my forehead to some stone. If I can remember
the music I will sing although the words
may be a little shaky. What is the thought
between two states? Which way should I turn? Deliver me,
I say to the sun, deliver me, to the moon.
It is the hour of deepest love, I walk
on the highway north of the city; I have abandoned
my Datsun, there is a field of wagons, there is
a valley of trees, an ice pond, a windmill. I walk
behind two calves, they are in a pickup, they slide
in terror, one is a dirty white, one is
a dirty black and white, their eyes are wild,
darkness will save them, sleep will save them. This way
is best, walking behind the calves. I have
my story. I have been walking here for an hour,
I am thinking of twilight. I am studying
the mountains of dust and the clouds. I am living
on the edge of total blackness. It is the time
it takes to walk two miles, at this time of year
at such and such a height in such a place.
I can see the yellow bands with borders
of red and purple, there is ice in the ditches

and wind inside the trees. I have my story
in case I'm stopped by a farmer or a state trooper,
in case a calf should splinter the wood, in case
Rabbi Akiba should stop me or Rabbi Judah,
asking about night and the first three stars,
testing me on purification and prayer,
in late February, outside Iowa City,
between one long-faced birthday and another.

MAKING THE LIGHT COME

My pen was always brown or blue, with stripes
of gold or silver at the shaft for streaks
of thought and feeling. I always wore the nib
on the left side. I was a mirror right-hander,
not a crazy twisted left-handed cripple,
trying to live in this world, his wrist half broken,
his shoulder shot through with pain. I lived by smiling,
I turned my face to the light—a frog does that,
not only a bird—and changed my metal table
three or four times. I struggled for rights to the sun
not only because of the heat. I wanted to see
the shadows on the wall, the trees and vines,
and I wanted to see the white wisteria
hanging from the roof. To sit half under it.
Light was my information. I was an immigrant
Jew in Boston, I was a Vietnamese
in San Jose, taking a quick lunch hour,
reading Browning—how joyous—I was worshiping
light three dozen years ago, it led me
astray, I never saw it was a flower
and darkness was the seed; I never potted
the dirt and poured the nutriments, I never
waited week after week for the smallest gleam.
I sit in the sun forgiving myself; I know
exactly when to dig. What other poet
is on his knees in the frozen clay with a spade
and a silver fork, fighting the old maples,
scattering handfuls of gypsum and moss, still worshiping?

IT WAS A RISING

It was a rising that brought the worms. They came
when the bodies came, the air was muddy, it was
a small mistake, the fingers were gone, the lips
were eaten away—though I love worms, they have
bags on their backs and pointed sticks, they come
by the thousands, they can clean a beach in an hour,
they can clean the ground of fruit and bottles,
paper and plastic. I was a worm once, I wore
an olive uniform, my specialty was Luckies,
I speared them by threes, I hooked a bone to a cup,
I caught the silver foil. The rain when it comes
forces the worms to the surface; that is another
rising but not as cataclysmic. Love
of one thing for another brought them up,
and love will bring them back. This is the flesh
that dies and this is the flesh that lives. The bone
at the base of the spine is called the almond, it is
the nucleus of our birth. I had my chance
when the worms were in the air. I went out swimming,
I started to float, I held my arms up sideways
and let myself be eaten. I lie on the beach
planning my future. I am a mile away
from the motors out there and I am a yard away
from the wet footprints. There is a bird half crying
and there are the waves half moaning, these are the sounds.
My nose alone is showing, most of my head
is buried, I should have a straw in my mouth
to breathe with and a periscope for my eye
to see the flags and see the derrick. I lie
in coldness, only my lips are burning; I crack

my blanket, I am free again, I rise
with sand on my shoulder, stomach, thighs. The calcium
ruins my arm; I try to wipe my back
and scream in pain; I crash into the water;
it is my justice there, in the blue, in the brown,
and I am happy. I find my stone with one breath
and rub the hatchings. It is a rolled-up scroll.
It is a book. I swim a few short lengths,
to Ireland and back, and end up walking the planks.
It is either the dream of Asbury Park
where it is built on clouds and there are cherubs
holding it end on end, or it is the city
itself, a state senator at one end,
a Confederate Legionnaire at the other,
in front of Perkins, with an unlined notebook,
ready for my own visionary window,
ready for a whole morning of sunlight and silence.

HOBBES

I am here again
walking through the long-term parking,
fighting the cold.
My mind is on Hobbes,
how he would fare on the small bus,
what luggage he would carry,
what he would do with his meanness.
I climb the two steps
and with my two red eyes
I make peace with the driver.
He will drop me at Piedmont
and I will drag myself to another counter
and another nasty and brutish computer.
All is poor and selfish
sayeth the monster;
only pride and fear of death
move us.
I hold my little contract in my hand
and walk down the ramp all bloody and sovereign.
I give my number up
and lie down in my padded seat
and tie myself in.
After a while I will be warm and happy,
maybe when breakfast is being carried in,
maybe when lunch;
and though Hobbes be with me
I will sing in my seat
and fall asleep over Kansas and southern Utah.
I will wake in the dark
and put my left shoe on over one mountain

and my right shoe on over another.
When the time comes
I will put my ugly suitcase in the narrow aisle
and wait for the bodies in front of me.
He who meets me, or she,
will know me by my flower
or the lines around my eyes
or my wolf walk,
and I will be his or hers forever,
three fulls days or more.
I will live in the sunshine
and breathe the air
and walk up and down the brown grass
and the white cement.
I will keep the beast
in my breast pocket
or the inside of my briefcase
next to the wine stain and the torn satin.
Going back
I will reconsider all my odd connections
and prepare for that long slow descent
through Altoona and Harrisburg and Whitehouse, New Jersey,
by whispering and sighing as always.
If Hobbes is there
we will get on the Long Term bus together
and I will be his—or hers—forever,
two or three minutes or more,
at least until we reach the shelters.
I have my number in one of my twelve pockets
and he has his.
He sings, you know, in bed,
and still plays tennis,
not so bad for an Englischer.
We drift apart on Route 22
and Route 24, going west and east.
This was a lifetime friend,

although we'd be apart sometimes for years.
I know no one
who loved his own head more.
I'll tell this story:
when Charles II turned against him
he stayed in bed for seven days and nights
murdering bishops.
He wrote a complete version of the *Iliad* and the *Odyssey*
when he was ninety.
He never gave up his wild attempt
to square the circle.
I make the turn on Route 78
singing Villa-Lobos.
I am a second soprano.
Life has been good the past eight years,
the past two months.
I write a letter to myself
on force and fraud in the twentieth century.
I write a long and bitter poem
against the sovereign,
a bastard, whoremonger and true asshole,
as always, my darling.

GRAPEFRUIT

I'm eating breakfast even if it means standing
in front of the sink and tearing at the grapefruit,
even if I'm leaning over to keep the juices
away from my chest and stomach and even if a spider
is hanging from my ear and a wild flea
is crawling down my leg. My window is wavy
and dirty. There is a wavy tree outside
with pitiful leaves in front of the rusty fence
and there is a patch of useless rhubarb, the leaves
bent over, the stalks too large and bitter for eating,
and there is some lettuce and spinach too old for picking
beside the rhubarb. This is the way the saints
ate, only they dug for thistles, the feel
of thorns in the throat it was a blessing, my pity
it knows no bounds. There is a thin tomato plant
inside a rolled-up piece of wire, the worms
are already there, the birds are bored. In time
I'll stand beside the rolled-up fence with tears
of gratitude in my eyes. I'll hold a puny
pinched tomato in my open hand,
I'll hold it to my lips. Blessed art Thou,
King of tomatoes, King of grapefruit. The thistle
must have juices, there must be a trick. I hate
to say it but I'm thinking if there is a saint
in our time what will he be, and what will he eat?
I hated rhubarb, all that stringy sweetness—
a fake applesauce—I hated spinach,
always with egg and vinegar, I hated
oranges when they were quartered, that was the signal
for castor oil—aside from the peeled navel

I love the Florida cut in two. I bend
my head forward, my chin is in the air,
I hold my right hand off to the side, the pinkie
is waving; I am back again at the sink;
oh loneliness, I stand at the sink, my garden
is dry and blooming, I love my lettuce, I love
my cornflowers, the sun is doing it all,
the sun and a little dirt and a little water.
I lie on the ground out there, there is one yard
between the house and the tree; I am more calm there
looking back at this window, looking up
a little at the sky, a blue passageway
with smears of white—and grey—a bird crossing
from berm to berm, from ditch to ditch, another one,
a wild highway, a wild skyway, a flock
of little ones to make me feel gay, they fly
down the thruway, I move my eyes back and forth
to see them appear and disappear, I stretch
my neck, a kind of exercise. Ah sky,
my breakfast is over, my lunch is over, the wind
has stopped, it is the hour of deepest thought.
Now I brood, I grimace, how quickly the day goes,
how full it is of sunshine, and wind, how many
smells there are, how gorgeous is the distant
sound of dogs, and engines—Blessed art Thou,
Lord of the falling leaf, Lord of the rhubarb,
Lord of the roving cat, Lord of the cloud.
Blessed art Thou oh grapefruit King of the universe,
Blessed art Thou my sink, oh Blessed art Thou
Thou milkweed Queen of the sky, burster of seeds,
Who bringeth forth juice from the earth.

A GARDEN

FOR GRETCHEN CARACAS
AND HOWARD ROGOVIN

This was my garden in 1985,
a piece of jade in a plastic cup, a bell jar
full of monarchs, a bottle of weeds, a Jew
hanging out of a glass, and one live flower,
a thin geranium in a jar of water,
the roots in slime, the brown leaves on the surface,
half reaching up for light and down for shadows.

I lived in the kitchen—all day—moving between
the stove and the sink, between the clock and the door.
I sat at the table reading, one foot over
a painted chair, an eye on the window, a pencil
pulling and pushing, helping me think, a bent
and withered daisy, dead for days, sticking out
of a brass vase, a postcard hanging over me.

I watered a few things, sometimes I moved the weeds
to the left, the jade to the right, sometimes I cleaned
the two sea shells and wiped a bottle, but mostly
I studied the Jew or lifted the jar of monarchs
and shook a little dust down. They were my tulips,
if anything was, my gory roses, just as
the twisted geranium was my hollyhock

and the bottle of weeds my phlox or my rhododendron.
I had no milkweed—there was a weakness. Next year
I'll plant a seed in a plastic glass. And I had
no parsley. Other than that I lived all summer
with a crowded windowsill and a dirty window;

as if I could find a little intelligence there
and a little comfort, as if I could find some refuge

between the shells and the coffee can, some pleasure
among the red petals, and even some in the leaves
that hang down over the sink; and as if I could find
five seconds of richness, say, as I bent my head
to taste the water, five seconds of pity, say,
as I wiped away the bugs, as I loosened a root,
or cleaned a leaf or found another bottle.

NO LONGER TERROR

In the sunset glow and early twilight and first star-sprinkling
I start to wander again. That way when the gloom
comes I can be in the hills, when darkness
is in the trees I can be in the open
with all that light going up and down, the pink
and yellow streaks, the variations, I can
come back to the lilacs and the wooden fence
before it's dark. I sit for three straight evenings
in a basket chair above the vines, my eyes
go over the roofs, I only look at shadows.
I spend my whole day waiting for this. There is
a bat and a dove. I have my choice; there are
the insects, it is May—the end of April—
there are no flowers but the tiny leaves
are curled and shining, as if there were; the grapes
will be here soon, they will be green at first
and then they will be black; the leaves will hide them,
the leaves will be like a roof. I will reach under
and pull at the stalks. I sit two feet away,
there is a ledge for my coffee, there is an urn
with dead leaves in the dirt. I put my book
on top of the leaves; on June twenty-first the light
will last another hour, it could be two
except for the clocks, there will be birds and bird song,
a little more wind than now, the train will roar
as it does now, only it will be daytime,
an hour from now—or two. I walk inside
when it gets dark. On my small porch there is
no lamp. I live by daylight, and dusk; Eurydice
is weeping on the radio, she has just

tramped on the snake and she is waiting to die;
Orpheus is singing in contrapunto.
Tomorrow I will look at the top three wires
and count the birds; the curtains in the living room,
I could watch that for hours. I put my head
on a heavy grey pillow—there are three others—I listen
to one thing and another, tomorrow morning
I will go back to my chair, life will be different,
it will be early, I will sit there reading
for hours, eating, answering the phone. At night
I'll wait for a certain light, I'll wait for the moon
to come between those houses, I'll wait for the sun
to leave, to have those two great hours, three,
if you count the shadows. What I will do depends
on the clouds and the dust. If there is a purple light
I will walk out again to see it, maybe
touch some bush or look at an insect still eating
and crawling at that hour, if it is a dull light
with a little yellow coming through—and green—
I will just sit there. I think the last thing I'd see
would be the clouds, a little yellow and pink
and a little whitish blue beyond the garages—
an hour earlier there. It is the darkness
I'm waiting for. Sometimes there is a glow
as if it were acid, sometimes it's black, that moonless
black, I feel my way, I stumble over
a plant and a table, I bang my knee on a trunk,
I trip on a rug. It is that last five minutes
I love, that last five seconds. I feel the wall
as I leave my chair—there I was sitting in darkness,
there I was starting to moan, I didn't even know,
I thought there still was daylight. I stood beside
the lamp, I rubbed the brass, I had to decide
whether or not to pull the chain. I stood
in front of the windows, there were thirteen plants
either hanging or on the window seats,

or on a table in front of the window seats,
a little forest; maybe there were eleven,
I watered them once a week; I saw their shapes,
even a little detail. There was some light
coming from the south, there were some stars,
some houses—somewhere—I looked out the side window,
I thought I saw some grapes, the leaves were brushing
against the screen, they were huge, there was a stick
holding the window up, there was a carpet
on top of the trunk—there may be just a board
from window to window, and not a window seat;
these plants will flower; outside the wind is blowing;
the last thing I see will be a green VW;
the last thing I see will be a cut-glass bottle,
blue I think; the Volkswagen is black,
the license plate is green; the last thing I'll do
is touch the plant above me; the last thing I'll do
is take my shoes off. Ah I still wear shoes,
though I am alone, I still wear socks and a shirt
with every button buttoned, I eat my meals
course by course, as if I were in a restaurant,
though I am alone, either thinking about the Greeks
or thinking about the bees gorging themselves
or—like tonight—thinking about the light,
how long it stayed, how long I will be in darkness,
how I couldn't lose a second, how sometimes I knelt
with my elbows on a chair to see the sky,
what joy it gave me, walking into the bedroom,
closing both doors, propping up the window.

NOBODY ELSE ALIVE

Nobody else alive knows the four heart sounds
and nobody touches the four soft places
and raises his wing to look for lice; and nobody
else sees himself as one of the skeletons
with another old white one in his arms
or looks for his keys in the long-term parking
and ends up with his pockets inside out
and his head pounding from the iron telephone pole.

Nobody is as clumsy.
Nobody breaks his darling's six new wineglasses
with a yellow sponge
or spills a pitcher of ice over his warm hand
or rubs his puzzled fingers over the butter
looking for paper.
Nobody carries his small notebook with such pure sorrow
and crosses his bloody femurs with such odd joy.

KNOWLEDGE FORWARDS AND
BACKWARDS

This was city living in the the 1930s,
making machine guns out of old inner tubes,
fighting above the garages. It was peaceful
killing and spying and maiming; sometimes we smoked
cigars, or roasted potatoes—we used gloves
to reach into the coals; sometimes I put
a cinder to my lips, a charred and filthy
piece of wood, then stirred through the fire hunting
my lost potato. We were not yet assimilated,
nothing fit us, our shoes were rotten; it takes
time to adjust to our lives, ten and twelve years
was not enough for us to be comfortable—
after a while we learn how to talk, how to cry,
what causes pain, what causes terror. Ah, we had
stars, in spite of the sulphur, and there was dreaming
as we came into the forties. I remember
the movies we went to—I am spending my life
accounting now, I am a lawyer, the one
with blood on his lips and cash in his pockets. I reach
across for the piece of paper, it is cardboard
from one blue shirt or another, there are columns,
I whistle as I study them. There is
a seal on the boardwalk, just about the size
of a tiny burro, the one I rode was blind
and circled left, the miniature golf is the same,
the daisies are there on the seventh hole, the palms
are crooked as always, the fences are rusted, the windmills
are painted blue and white, as always, the ocean

is cold, I hated the ocean, Poseidon bounced me
over and over, I was gasping then,
trying to get a breath, and I am gasping
now, my rib is broken, or bruised, the muscle
inside the bone, or over the bone. I have
a hundred things to think about, my mind
goes back, it is a kind of purse, nothing
is ever lost. I wait for the pain to change
to pleasure, after a while my lips will stop moving,
I will stop moaning, I will start sleeping, one day
there is an end, even if at this end
there is lucidity and gruesome recollection
and I am paying for every red mark and blue mark.
I have the calendar in front of me;
I have the pencil at my lips, but no one
can live in place of us, there is no beast
on the seventh hole to save us; the grass is false,
it is a kind of cellophane, it is
produced in shops, above garages, maybe
in spare bedrooms or out of car trunks; there is
no spirit with her finger on her forehead
and her mouth open; there is no voice for sobbing
so we can sob with it a little, although—
and I am only beginning to feel this—I am
accumulating—what could I call it, a shadow?—
I am becoming a kind of demon, you turn
into a demon, with knowledge forwards and backwards,
backwards, forwards, you develop a power,
you develop a look, you go for months
with sight, with cunning, I see it in older men,
older women, a few of them, you stand
at some great place, in front of the Port Authority
or facing the ocean, you see the decade in front of you,
you see yourself out there, you are a swimmer
in an old wool suit, you are an angry cabbie,
you are a jeweler, you are a whore, the smell

of burned pretzels is everywhere, you walk
backwards and forwards, there is a point where the knot
is tied, you touch your fingers, you make a cage,
you make a roof, a steeple, at last you walk
forwards and backwards, your shirt is thin, your elbows
are getting longer, you are a type of demon,
you can go forth and forth, now it's the ocean
now it's the Port Authority, now you are sixty,
standing behind the pretzel man, amazed
at the noise around you, amazed at the clothes, amazed
at the faces; now you are twelve, you stand in a little
valley of water, you study the sand, you study
the sky, it was a violent journey, you end up
forgetting yourself, you stand at some place, there are
thousands of places, you stand in the Chrysler Building
beside the elevators, you stand in a lookout
on Route 78, you stand in the wooden post office
in Ocean Grove, in front of the metal boxes;
it is a disgrace to dance there, it is shameful
snapping your fingers, if we could just be singers
we'd walk down Main Street singing, no one as yet
has done this, three and four abreast, the language
could be Armenian, it could be Mohawk—
that is a dream too, something different from Whitman
and something different from Pound. What a paradise,
in front of the Quaker Inn, the women are watching,
I'm singing tenor, someone is taking a picture.
For me, when there is no hierarchy, for me,
when there is no degradation, when the dream
when lying is the same as the dream when walking,
when nothing is lost, when I can go forth and forth,
when the chain does not break off, that is paradise.

TWO MOONS

I'm looking at the moon, I'm half resting
on my right knee until the water settles.
There is a tree in the upper left-hand corner,
there is a house beside it. No one is watching,
I'm dying out here in the cold, I move my leg,
my knee is muddy, I shift to the other knee,
there are some waves between the cracks, there is
some grass inside the windows, it is marsh grass,
the blades are thick and sharp; I lean half over
to see my face, it is that Jewish face,
or Slavic face, that Spanish, I am grieved
by the lines around the eyes and by the fat
around the neck, around the chin; I stir
the water a little, near the mouth, a light
is coming on somewhere, someone is watching
me having my heart attack or dropping my key;
the moon is in its final phase, it drips
thick milk, there is a branch that looks like a calf,
it suckles the moon, it digs its feet in the ground,
its eyes are wild, the slaver is on its chin;
I have been still enough, I stand on my feet,
I stamp a little, the light goes out, I howl
silently, silently, I have learned that from dogs,
though I have learned when not to howl, I learned that
from parents and teachers, clerks and principals,
dentists and rabbis, doctors and lawyers—I hear
baying in Chile and baying in Africa,
men look up and see the moon, they scream
from pain, their backs are smashed, their faces are swollen,
their eardrums are broken, their genitals are purple,

there are welts from their shoulders to their buttocks,
they have been drinking gasoline, it is
too brilliant to bear, it should be dark, such beauty
is agonizing. There is a telephone wire
above the house, and a cigarette butt on the chimney
beside the grass, wet and useless. I drop
a stone in for a hurricane, there was
too much of crystal, I will leave when the sirens
go off, there will be a truck or an ambulance,
I will play footsie with the girl beside me,
she is nine, ah those are the girls that know me,
and love me and understand me, their poor mothers
are nervous, helpless. I am thinking of Yeats,
and Keats and Pound, on beauty. Somewhere a general,
somewhere a tall policeman is looking at the moon,
he wipes away some blood from his boot, there is
a tooth, and a piece of tongue, caught in the laces,
he waits for his daughter, she is nine, he gives her
a gentle touch, how gentle he is. Somewhere
up there the dust is falling, I have read it,
somewhere valleys and mountains, somewhere lake beds—
Darling Li Po, I bend my lips to the moon,
I wait for the tide, I touch myself with mud,
the forehead first, the armpits, behind the knees,
clothes or no clothes; now I walk on my face,
I had to do that, now I walk on the wires,
now I am on the moon, I am standing
between two moons, always there are two moons,
one for us and one for them, we know it,
visiting famous hills, following shadows,
believing in water, bowing to sparrows, bowing
to white deer, refusing to shame the spirit.

LYRIC

I wonder who has pissed here
and stared—like me—at those wild petunias
or touched a purple leaf from that small pear tree.

Has anyone lain down here
beside those red peppers
or under those weak elm withers
standing in shame there?

Dear God of that grape,
has anyone snapped off a little curlicue
to see if it's wood or wire
or stripped the bark off those thick vines
and leaned against that broken fence?

Has anyone put some old parsley in his mouth
to see what the taste is
or lifted a rose mum to his face
to see if he'll live forever?

MY FAVORITE FAREWELL

There is a kind of mop hanging down from the tree.
It is a willow. It has its own sad branches
somewhere. There is a huge Greek crypt
in front of the tree and there are stairs going down
to some kind of darkness. In the other corner
there are three cypresses—they stand alone
against a light blue sky—and there are flowers
around the crypt and bushes on the hillside.

Sadness is everywhere. Hector is holding
his wife's thin wrist and staring into her eyes.
Her hand is hanging loosely on his neck
and she is holding back her tears. A plume
is sitting on his helmet and a beard
is hanging from his neck; his skirt is made
of gorgeous pelts and there are purple thongs
around his leg tied in a little ribbon.

What else? The nurse is holding the baby. He is
enormous. Andromache's robes are flowing.
There are pompoms on her shoes and disks
holding her sleeves up, and her girdle. Her hair
is wavy and hanging to her waist but the nurse's
is just below her fluted ear. Hector
is resting his right hand on a shield—it's more
like a lopsided wheel. He doesn't have a spear.

What else? There is a pond underneath the cypresses
and they are on a hill. There is an effort
at vegetation beside the pond. Hector's

sleeves are rolled up. Andromache is in motion.
The crypt is out of proportion; the background is missing
on the left side; the steps seem to go up
instead of down; there is a violet filagree
behind the steps; the pillars are covered with disks.

It is my favorite farewell. As I watch it
I know Achilles will tear his helmet off
and drag his body through the dust, and I know
his enemies will spit on him and stab
him and the dogs will feed on his blood. I pay
attention to these things. It is the only
life we have. I am happy to be here
in front of the silk work and embroidery

watching them say goodbye. They will have to
make do with their sentiments and banalities.
That is all they have. Their hands are clumsy.
Their hills are unconvincing. Their clouds are muddy.
They are lucky to have the cypresses
and they are lucky that there's a streak of blue
behind the willow. I press against the glass.
There is a nail stuck inside the silk

that adds another oddness to the painting,
that makes it flat and distant and ruins illusion—
if there was any illusion—although it may
have fallen from the backing and slid down
the sky and down the shield and through the ribbons
into the dirt. I kiss the baby goodbye.
I kiss the nurse goodbye. The snow is falling
and I will be walking in the street half buried

inside my overcoat. I remember
the ending now. They put his white bones
in a golden box and wrapped it in soft purple

before they covered it up with dirt and stones.
That was a nice farewell—Andromache sobbing,
Hecuba howling, Helen tearing her hair out.
I think it is the cypresses that moved me
the most although it is the mop-faced willow

that is the center of the grief. The cypresses
are like a chorus standing on top of the sky
and moaning—they are moaning about the wind
and moaning about the narrow steps; they sit
on the edge of a hill, they hardly are planted, they whisper
about Achilles: "Think of Achilles," they whisper.
"Think of his tapered spear, think of his shield
with three kinds of metal, thicker than a wrist,

heavier than a door, think of lifting it
and holding it up with one huge hand while the other
searches the air and dances"—I find it moving
in spite of the stiffness and pallor of the figures,
in spite of the missing leg and floating branches.
It is my fondness for those souls. It is
my love of childish trees and light blue skies
and flowing robes. I have to be forgiven.

FOR ONCE

It was in southern Florida I reached
my foot across to trap a soul. He strayed
from one orange tile to another; he would live
for twenty seconds under my shoe, then run
to his door and pant an hour or two. I watched him
climb his wall. He turned his head and stared.
He lifted one gluey leg, then another.

He was from Enoch, one of the little false ones
full of mathematics and wizardry,
a slave to the moon. We yodeled and sang together—
it was like scraping chalk—I touched his throat.
It was translucent. I could see the spiders
going down his gullet. "Just one more song," I sang,
and there, two blocks from the ocean, six thousand years
into our era, we stood on the street and shouted.

There was a sunset somewhere. Someone cranked
a window open, as if to listen. Beyond that
there were our noises, an airplane droning, a car
beginning a trip, a baby screaming, a woman
yelling in Spanish. We stood beside each other—
if you could call that standing, and speculated.
We were mediators. I rubbed his head
and his yellow eyes began to close. The two of us
were getting ready for something—I could tell that—
before we lost each other.
                              I was left
with the bougainvillaeas and the narrow sidewalk

and the chain-link fences and the creeping vines.
I kept the music secret, walking south
on the left side of the road, beside the mosses.
Our sound was southern, mixed a little with Spanish,
mixed a little with French, and Creole. For once
there was no Polish, or German. I was adjusting
to the dunes and swamps, although there was some forties,
and thirties too; the last thing I did was whistle
and ring the fences. I was alone now and wandered
up and down those streets. I thought of the tail;
I thought of the heart. I don't know about the heart,
how many chambers there are, how cold it gets,
where it shunts the blood to, what the pulse is,
if it's a *clumsy* heart, if it can love
like ours can, if it can be grown again, if food
destroys it and exercise renews it, if memory
can make it flutter, if passion can make it flow.

This I thought about going south on one street
and east on another, picking up coconuts
and holding them to my ear, tearing the fronds up
and wearing them like a shawl. It was a kind
of happiness, shrieking and hollering in the tropics,
watching my skin grow dry and my blood grow thin,
wandering through a forest of cypress roots,
finding someone that old and wise. I loved it.

STOLEN FACE

Piazza St. Andreas, Lucca, Italy

There is a face stolen from the twelfth century
I come back to over and over. I wait for
the train for hours and hours, sometimes it's raining,
sometimes the sun is beating down—although I
like to wait for evening, there's that golden
light you get in some of the painters, cities
are in the distance, trees are small but clear,
there are tiny churches and walled-in saints
and miniature rivers and miniature clouds and mountains.
The eyes are a little crossed and the head is thrust
forward, in either stupidity or terror—
I'll say that now—although it could be curiosity
that made him stretch his neck like that. There is no
neck, of course, there is a moon face, a disk,
that is the last link in a frieze, the bottom
of an arch—I think it was taken from something else
and put there—and it matches another disk
at the other side of the arch, although the other
face for me is insignificant
compared to the first. For one thing the stone lion
underneath it *hides* the face and even
casts a little shadow over it
in almost every light. There are *two* lions,
one on the left and one on the right, each of them
is standing over a man, their looks are vague
and even aloof; it is the look of a cat
straddling a rat, he knows every move but seems
almost bored. The man on the right is terrified,
his eyes are bulging, his hands are holding on,
one to the lion's leg, one to his paw;

the one on the left is twisted sideways, his right hand
is holding the lion's mouth, his left the paw—
the very same place. The hair on the left is wavy,
the man's hair and the lion's; the hair on the right
is curled, all of it, mane and beard and forehead;
and there are other lions—with rats—in sets,
just like this one; one has a fat stone snake
under his belly, one has another lion,
a mirror lion, biting and snarling. The face
on the right, above the lion, has a pipe
coming out of the mouth, and he is cross-eyed.
I don't know if it's part of a drainage system,
a kind of fountain, or a huge cigar,
either way the face is ugly. The eyes,
as I say, are crossed, and the cheeks are puffed a little
from blowing out water—or smoke—and the soul is drowned.

I know there are other faces like these faces
all over Lucca. In St. Martin's alone I counted
fourteen faces though most of them were covered
by scaffolding and netting. There are faces
like it on St. Michael facing the mountain
and there is a face on the front of St. Christopher
that stares at the sky as if it were drunk on sleeping
though none of them has the spirit of the one face.
They look as if they were being punished. One
has his mouth open, his teeth are showing, the lines
are carved in his jowls and forehead; one is screaming
because of some hidden terror, one is straining
with all his might to hold a pillar up.
They are like masks, these faces, carrying life
and death like masks do, they are like drawings, one line
crossing another line, just that, and the flesh
is suddenly there. There is a book I love,
a face with two lines on it showed it to me,
a face fat from sitting. It is a book

showing the faces of Jesus for five hundred years,
including the Botticelli at Bergamo,
including the Veronese at the Louvre,
including the Juan Juares at Madrid,
sometimes tender, sometimes thin and careworn,
sometimes broken with pain. Sodoma's Christ
is silent, the lips are open, horror and sadness
are in his eyes; Guercino's Christ is foolish,
huge drops of blood are trickling down his face,
his eyes are looking up, he is insipid
and full of self-pity. The Christ of Jan Van Eyck
is matter-of-fact and unemotional,
it is a portrait, someone stood in front of him
and stared at the window. Giorgione's Christ is thoughtful,
his eyes are full of light, his look is gentle,
the crown doesn't pierce his brow, there is no anguish,
nothing is sickly. It is the opposite.

Now I have eighty-nine steps to climb. Each landing
is another burden—you should forgive me—I gasp
at number four, at number five. How crazy
it is to climb someone else's steps. I'm tired
of always living this way. At every window
I touch my throat. What was it like to have
your own city? What is that round face doing
above its Renault? What is the rat doing staring
down at the shoemaker, down at the street cleaner?
This is my evening: I light the stove and boil
a little tea. I stare at St. Michael's—I live
behind the façade. I can see the steps
above the roof. It is as if the ceiling
were meant to be raised. St. Michael has his arm up,
he is letting the sun down. He has a wand,
his two assistants are playing horns. The snow
is always on the hills. I start to break
the sticks, we need some kindling, we need some paper,

the wood is hard and green, the chimney is crude,
it is the sky we heat, a little smoke
among the stars. I fool myself by blowing
air on the coals. I make a wobbly face
of smoke and fire. I put the nose in. It is
a Spanish face, ascetic and melancholic
and overcome with grief; it is a Dutch face,
almost coarse, wholesome and unimaginative,
not one nimbus, every line exact.
I stare at myself, the trick is finally to do it
without a mirror. The teeth have separated
a little, the hair is whiter, the neck is thicker,
but who would know that in this light? I put
the lines in the cheek—I think I like them wavy—
I am the one from Asbury Park, I am
the one from New Orleans, the one from France,
the one from Philadelphia. I believe
the Jews of Russia came afrom Asia, but the Jews
of Poland came from Spain and Africa.

Tomorrow I will wake up freezing. I'll get there
before the market is open, it is two blocks
east and two blocks south; the moon at six
in the morning is tired, his eyes are closed, the bulging
one follows my eyes, there is a cast in *his* eyes—
were they not crossed? He stares all night. The crudeness
must get to him. I listen. I learned that idleness
from Moses. I listen for a sound but nothing
comes—it is too hard to speak. I show him
my sack of old clothes, he likes that, I show him my permits
to trade with the East, I show him my medicines—
I am allowed to practice—I show him my bills
of lading—they are just old receipts but he is
impressed. I sit on the hood to hear his sermon—
ah, I will convert, believe me. This is the last
time we will see each other, or maybe I'll pass

him again with pears in one hand, wine in the other,
and only remember when I am walking past
the furniture store and stop to look in the window
or when I am sitting at one of the metal tables
under a striped umbrella, my pen half balanced
as if it were a spear, my paper white
from the morning sun. If he is a Lombard I
am happy, if he is something Byzantine I
am happy too. If we are allowed one face
it must be this one, hard and coarse as the eyes are,
thick as the nose is, round as the head is. I make
my way to the station walking like a lobster,
with ninety pounds on my back; the last thing I did
was visit that square again. I keep coming back
as if I would learn something, as if the next time
there would be a disclosure. It took one second
and everything there was to know I knew.
Now I'm leaving. I walk down some steps. I'm dragging
my body through a tunnel. I'm counting to fifty
to make the load lighter. Now I'm counting to thirty.
I check my two main pockets. I shift the burden.
I practice a verb. I check my shoes for water.
I check my brain for air. I follow the arrows.

STEPS

There are two hundred steps between my house
and the first café. It is like climbing a ladder.
I gasp and pant as if I were pulling a mule,
as if I were carrying a load of dirt. I do
the journey twice—I left the key in the car
the first time down. There is another hill
above the first—the road to the car—another
one hundred steps. But I was born in Pittsburgh
and I know hills; I know that second rise
after a leveling off; I know the gentleness
between the two pair of steps, I know the wear
at the center, if it is stone, the soft splinters,
if it is wood, and I know the broken spaces,
the rhythm stoppers—railroad ties—but even
worse, I know the broken heights, four inches
and then a foot, and then another foot,
or fourteen inches, and the curves that carry you
around and around. There is a street on the South Side—
Pittsburgh again—that goes up hundreds of feet.
It is a stairs. I walked until my thighs
had turned to stone; and there were walkways like that
on the side of streets and cars that only made it
partway up, some turned around, some facing
the houses, abandoned cars. I am in Samos,
a village called Stavrinidhes, halfway up
the mountain of Ampelos. The town of Ampelos
is two miles away, a forty-minute walk.
I sit all day and watch. The sea is on my left.
The hills are all around me. Today is the walk
to Manolates, an hour and a half by foot,

a little less by car; it is a mulepath
up and down the ridges. I like the streets
in Ampelos. You climb for fifteen minutes,
your legs go slower and slower; this time there is
the long slope, the slant between the steps,
no relief at all, and there are two steps
twenty-five inches apiece, and there is a stairs
with a tree at the top, it is a kind of pyramid,
a kind of throne, the tree is a king, it sits there
painted white, and there is a waterfall
of steps, it almost pours. I touch a window
on my left, I touch a curtain, there is a trumpet vine
in front of the house, there is wisteria—
a limb that stretches half a block—I touch
a cactus, I touch a telephone pole, I reach
the hill above the town. The thing about climbing
is how you give up. I sit on a rock. I am
in front of a mountain. There's a white horse behind me,
there's a two-foot cypress beside me, it's already
burdened with balls. I am waiting for Hera,
she was born on this island. Zeus must have roared
on every mountain, he must have lifted a pine tree
to make a bed for them, or scooped out a valley.
Ah, Lord, she was too full of anger. The clock
says something on one side, something else on the other.
It rises above the houses. There are some towns
in Pennsylvania like this, and West Virginia;
I have sat on mountains. Imagine Zeus
in West Virginia, imagine the temple to Hera
in Vandergrift, P.A. My heart is resting,
my back feels good, my breathing is easy. I think
of all my apartments, all that climbing; I reach
for a goldenrod, I reach for a poppy, the cross
is German more than Greek, our poppies are pale
compared to these. I gave up on twenty landings,
I gave up in Paris once, it was impossible,

you reach a certain point, it is precise,
you can't go further; sometimes it's shameful, you're in
the middle of a pair of stairs, you bow
your head, your hand is on the rail; your breath
is hardly coming; sometimes you run to the top
so you can stop at the turning, then your legs burn,
sometimes they shake, while you are leaning over
and staring down the well or holding your arm
against the wall. Sometimes the stairs are curved,
that makes a difference, sometimes the risers are high,
sometimes there are too many turns, your knees
cannot adjust in time. Sometimes it's straight up,
landing after landing. Like a pyramid.
You have to lean into the steps, you have to
kneel a little to stop from falling backwards.
I turn around to look at the mountain. There is
a little path going up, some dirt and stones;
it would take two more hours. The wind is almost
roaring here—a gentle roar—the ocean
is green at first, then purple. I can see Turkey.
Who knows that I have given up? I hear
two women talking, I hear a rooster, there is
the back of a chimney, seventy bricks, there is
a cherry tree in blossom, there is a privy,
three hundred bricks to a side, there is a cat
moaning in Greek. You would look at the cherry tree,
you would rest your feet on a piece of marble,
you would be in semi-darkness; there are
dark pink cherries on the roof, the bowl
is sitting on a massive base, the floor
is dirt, there is no door. I wave to a donkey,
I read his lips, his teeth are like mine, I walk
to the left to see the oven, I count the bricks,
I look at the clock again, I chew my flower.